# A Crazy Day at the Critter Café

by Barbara Odanaka

illustrated by Lee White

SCHOLASTIC INC.
New York Toronto London Auckland
Sydney Mexico City New Delhi Hong Kong

For Paul—B. O.

For Lisa—L. W.

ISBN: 978-0-545-23603-4

12 11 10 9 8 7 6 5 4 3 2 1                     10 11 12 13 14 15/0

Printed in the U.S.A.                     08

This edition first printing, January 2010

Book design by Debra Sfetsios
The text for this book is set in Kosmik.
The illustrations for this book are rendered in mixed media.

It looked like a pile of mashed potatoes,

smelled of fish and stewed tomatoes.

It was sleeping soundly—snoring, too—

when it opened its eyes and said,

"Moo?"

"WOW!" said Cow. "I missed the bus?
And now it's just the *three* of us?
Toss me an apron! Show me the way!

This ol' cow is HERE TO STAY!"

They danced and hugged,
clapped and cheered,
until they spotted
something **WEIRD.**

"HOORAY!" cried the waiter.
"YIPPEE!" sang the cook.
"We're free at last!"
"We're off the hook!"

The animals shuffled, shoulders sagging.
Tails tucked, feathers dragging.

"C'mon, critters," their driver said.

"Engine's fixed." And off they sped.

And don't come
back here **anymore.**"

"Now listen here, all of you:

This café is **NOT** a zoo.

Pay your bill,
then out the door.

the waiter staggered
to his knees.
"Achoo!"

Out flew two buttered peas.

Wiping **cupcake** from his eyes,
covered in ketchup,
milk, and fries,

Ol' Jumbo tried to toot his horn. What popped out? A cob of corn.

A strawberry sundae doused a yak.

A snail flicked kale off his back.

Maple syrup, cottage cheese,

splattered chicks and chimpanzees.

Spaghetti and meatballs, root beer floats,

dropped and plopped on pigs and goats.

The waiter's tray flipped through the air, launching food—

E-V-E-R-Y-W-H-E-R-E!

**"DUDE!"**

With tail twitching, Cow zoomed in.

**"SHE'S LOST CONTROL!"** screamed a pangolin.

Cow lurched this way,
then lurched that,
then crashed into the waiter— **SPLAAAAAAT!**

"Settle down.

Just eat your food.

It might **improve your** atti—"

**"Stop already!"**

the waiter said,

his tray seesawing

above his head.

"What's this green stuff?
Is it ... **MOLD?**"

"Mine is icky!"

"Mine's too sticky!"

"Hush!" said the waiter.

"You're much too picky."

"I can't eat this—it's too hot!"

"I want what that otter's got!"

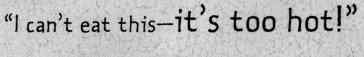

"Mine's too warm!"

"Mine's too cold!"

Raccoons crawled
atop their chairs.

Cow skateboarded
down the stairs.
The waiter
scrambled
this way
and that.

"You forgot ME," squeaked a rat.

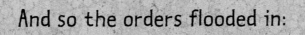
And so the orders flooded in:

"Apple pie!" said a pangolin.

An ostrich squawked:

"Cherry strudel!"

"Chips and salsa!" yipped a poodle.

"Quiet, please,"

the waiter said.

"Just sit down.

We'll get you fed."

Above the din, a wolf pup howled,

"Oh, dear me, my tummy growled!"

Macaws, turtles, lizards, lambs,

penguins, zebras, kangaroos, rams . . .

So many creatures poured off the bus,

**screeching, squawking—what a fuss!**

Swish,
**zoom,**
swish.

Clickety-
clack!

Cow spun round,

then **twirled back.**

She was zooming past the apple fritters

when through the door
came a rush of critters.

The raccoons hollered,

"Feed us now!"

when through the door

rolled Skateboard Cow.

Toot, **toot,** toot!

Boom, **boom, boom!**

Tubas and bass drums rattled the room.

"Hey there, waiter.

We need some grub.

Our bus broke down.

We're starving, Bub!"

The waiter jumped up,

menus in hand,

when through the door came
an **elephant band.**

**IT WAS A QUIET MORNING** at the Critter Café.

The cook was dozing in his cheese soufflé.

The waiter was whistling sleepy tunes

when through the door walked **five raccoons.**

. . . was that.

Cow's Café

The cook and waiter, too shocked to speak,

shot out the door like a lightning streak.

"But Cook!" called Cow.
"You forgot your hat!"
She tried it on. And *that* . . .